A MONSTER STORY

Big Lips
and Hairy
Arms

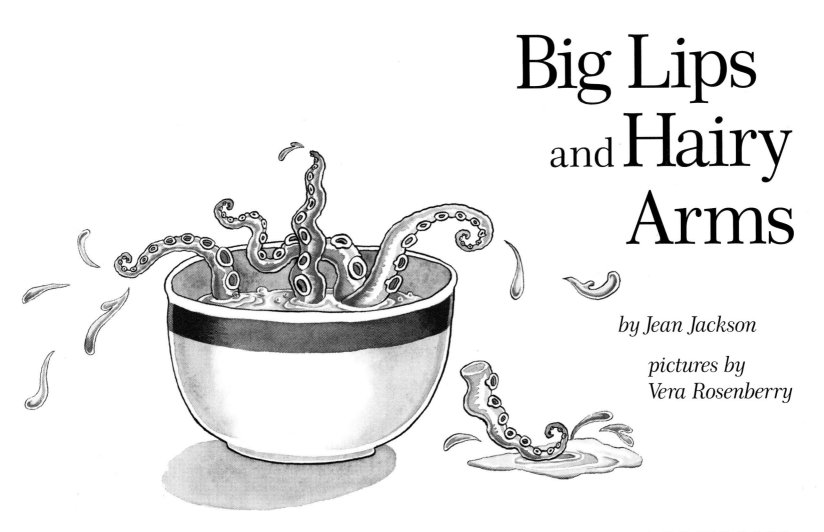

by Jean Jackson

pictures by
Vera Rosenberry

A DK INK BOOK
DK PUBLISHING, INC.

For my mother, Sally Candiotti
Thank you for your love and generosity.
and
For Margaret Jackson
Thank you for James.—JJ

To Veta, who is in the telephone business, sort of,
and who may find a laugh here.—VR

A Richard Jackson Book

DK Publishing, Inc.
95 Madison Avenue
New York, New York 10016

Visit us on the World Wide Web at http://www.dk.com

Library of Congress Cataloging-in-Publication Data
Jackson, Jean.
Big lips and hairy arms / by Jean Jackson ; illustrated by Vera Rosenberry. — 1st ed.
p.   cm.
Summary: While having dinner together, two monsters get scared when they start receiving mysterious telephone calls.
ISBN 0-7894-2521-1
[1. Monsters—Fiction.]   I. Rosenberry, Vera, ill.   II. Title.
PZ7.J13623Bi   1998   [E]—dc21   97-43605   CIP   AC

The text of this book is set in 16 point Primer.
The illustrations are ink and watercolor paintings reproduced in full color.
Printed and bound in U.S.A.

First Edition, 1998
2   4   6   8   10   9   7   5   3   1

One cold, windy evening, two monsters sat in front of a crackling fire, slurping tentacle stew and crunching on caterpillar crisps.

"Thank you for inviting me to dinner," Nelson said. "By the way, this stew is disgusting!"

Thorndike turned pink with pleasure. "I thought you would like it," he said.

Brrring-a-ling-ling!

Nelson jumped. "What's that?" he asked.

Thorndike pulled a sleek black handset out of his pocket. "It's my new cell phone," he replied. "ThriftyMart had a big sale. I bought two—one for me and one for my mother for her birthday."

When the phone rang again, Thorndike pulled out the antenna and pushed a button. "Hello?" he said.

A deep raspy voice replied, "I have big lips and hairy arms, and I'm only five blocks away!"

"Big what?" Thorndike asked. "Harry who?" But the caller had hung up.

"Who was that?" Nelson asked.

"I don't know," Thorndike replied. "The connection was bad. But I'm sure I've heard that voice before!"

"Oh," Nelson said. Then his arm shot out in front of Thorndike's nose as he pointed across the room. "What's that?"

"What?" Thorndike said. "Where? I don't see anything."

When he turned back around, his bowl of caterpillar crisps was mysteriously empty. And Nelson's cheeks were so stuffed he looked like he was trying to blow up a balloon.

Thorndike asked Nelson if he wanted to play Pin the Teeth on the Dragon. Nelson's mouth was too full to speak. He just smiled a little and nodded.

The dragon had one tooth on its tail, six in its left nostril, and three hanging from its chin when the phone rang again.

"Hello?" Thorndike answered.
And the same deep raspy voice replied, "I have big lips and hairy arms, and I'm only *three* blocks away!"

A chill went up Thorndike's spine. "Who is this?" he demanded. "What do you want?" But the caller did not reply.

"A prankster," Thorndike said to Nelson. Nelson didn't answer. He couldn't—his mouth was full again.

Outside, a gust of wind shrieked through the trees. The lights flickered, and rain broke against the windows like tiny transparent eggs. Thorndike carried the empty dinner dishes back into the kitchen while Nelson flipped through a copy of *Monster Monthly*.

Then the phone rang again,
and Nelson's dog, Dot, started
making strange sounds, like
an old car trying to start.

Thorndike came running out of the kitchen.

"What's that noise?" he asked.

"It's Dot," Nelson replied. "She's growling."

Brrring-a-ling-ling! The phone rang a second time.

Thorndike turned to Nelson. "You answer it," he said.

Very slowly Nelson picked up the phone.
He held it so Thorndike could hear too.
"Hello?" he said.

And the same deep raspy voice replied, "I have big lips and hairy arms, and I'm only *one* block away!" Then *click,* the caller hung up.

The back of Nelson's neck broke out in goose bumps. "Oh, wow!" he said, pointing to his watch. "Look at the time! I better be heading home!"

"Nelson," Thorndike said. "If you go home now, I will never ever ever make you caterpillar crisps again!"

Nelson rubbed his stomach.
"I don't like them so much anymore," he said.

"Nelson . . ." Thorndike warned.
"Okay, okay, I'll stay," Nelson said.
The phone rang again.

Thorndike took a deep breath. He wiped his brow. He rubbed his sweaty palms on his pants legs. Then he answered the phone.

"Hello?"

"Is this the Thorndike P. Finklemeyer residence?" a voice asked.

"Yes," Thorndike replied.

"Good!" the deep raspy voice replied. "Because I have big lips and hairy arms, and I'm *right across the street*!"

Thorndike screamed and dropped the phone. Then he rushed to the front door and locked it.

Nelson pulled the drapes. Dot started to growl again.
"Stop that!" Nelson said.

Then he noticed that he and Dot were all alone in the living room. "Thorndike, Thorndike, where are you?" he cried.

A small grunt came from somewhere behind Nelson. He whirled around and saw a long green toe poking out from under the couch.

Nelson grabbed it and pulled. Out came Thorndike.

Suddenly something went *bump* on the front porch. Thorndike and Nelson grabbed each other and squeezed.

There was a small *click*, then the doorknob began to slowly turn—

"This can't be happening!" Thorndike whispered. "I locked that door!"

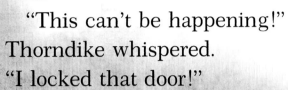

"Stop squeezing so tight," Nelson whispered back. "I can't breathe!"

The door burst open, and a great ugly monster rushed in. "Want to know what I can *do* with my big lips and hairy arms?" it asked.

Then it grabbed Thorndike and kissed him with its big lips and hugged him with its hairy arms.

"Mother!" Thorndike exclaimed. "Why didn't you tell me you were coming over?"

"What?" Thorndike's mother asked as she patted the cell phone clipped to her belt. "Didn't you get my phone calls?"